W9-AKV-612

Witch Switch

To Mandy and Ian, who are full of
all sorts of tricks and treats!—NK
For Cristina, keeper of the
skeleton keys to Halloween—J&W

GROSSET & DUNLAP
Published by the Penguin Group
Penguin Group (USA) Inc., 375 Hudson Street,
New York, New York 10014, U.S.A.
Penguin Group (Canada), 90 Eglinton Avenue East, Suite 700,
Toronto, Ontario, Canada M4P 2Y3
(a division of Pearson Penguin Canada Inc.)
Penguin Books Ltd, 80 Strand, London WC2R 0RL, England
Penguin Ireland, 25 St Stephen's Green, Dublin 2, Ireland
(a division of Penguin Books Ltd)
Penguin Group (Australia), 250 Camberwell Road,
Camberwell, Victoria 3124, Australia
(a division of Pearson Australia Group Pty Ltd)
Penguin Books India Pvt Ltd, 11 Community Centre,
Panchsheel Park, New Delhi - 110 017, India
Penguin Group (NZ), Cnr Airborne and Rosedale Roads,
Albany, Auckland 1310, New Zealand
(a division of Pearson New Zealand Ltd)
Penguin Books (South Africa) (Pty) Ltd, 24 Sturdee Avenue,
Rosebank, Johannesburg 2196, South Africa

Penguin Books Ltd, Registered Offices:
80 Strand, London WC2R 0RL, England

If you purchased this book without a cover, you should be aware that
this book is stolen property. It was reported as "unsold and destroyed" to
the publisher, and neither the author nor the publisher has received any
payment for this "stripped book."

The scanning, uploading, and distribution of this book via the Internet
or via any other means without the permission of the publisher is illegal
and punishable by law. Please purchase only authorized electronic editions
and do not participate in or encourage electronic piracy of copyrighted
materials. Your support of the author's rights is appreciated.

Text copyright © 2006 by Nancy Krulik. Illustrations copyright © 2006 by
John and Wendy. All rights reserved. Published by Grosset & Dunlap, a
division of Penguin Young Readers Group, 345 Hudson Street, New York,
New York 10014. GROSSET & DUNLAP is a trademark of Penguin Group
(USA) Inc. Printed in the U.S.A.

Library of Congress Control Number: 2005033370

ISBN 0-448-44330-9   10 9 8 7 6 5 4 3 2 1

NORMAL PUBLIC LIBRARY
NORMAL, ILLINOIS
DISCARD

Witch Switch

by Nancy Krulik • illustrated by John & Wendy

Grosset & Dunlap

Chapter 1

HALLOWEEN PARADE
THIS FRIDAY

The big orange and black sign was the first thing Katie Carew and her best friend Suzanne Lock saw as they walked onto the school playground on Monday morning.

"I can't wait for Halloween!" Katie exclaimed. "Trick-or-treating is the best way to celebrate a holiday."

"You say that about going caroling at Christmas," Suzanne reminded her. "And the Fourth of July fireworks, and Easter egg hunts, and . . ."

"I guess I just like holidays," Katie said with a giggle.

"Have you decided what you're going to dress up as this year?" Suzanne asked.

Katie nodded excitedly. "I'm going as a chocolate brown and white cocker spaniel."

"You're going as Pepper, *again*?" Suzanne said with a sigh. Pepper was Katie's cocker spaniel. "You did that last year."

"I know," Katie said. "And it was a lot of fun. Pepper loved seeing me dressed like that. Besides, this year I'm doing something different. I'm going to carry around a big cardboard bone."

"You should think of something more original," Suzanne told her. "You'll never win a prize at the Halloween parade with a costume like that."

"Well, do you have a better idea?" Katie asked.

Suzanne nodded. "Yes!" she exclaimed. "We could go as witches."

Katie frowned. "What's so original about being witches on Halloween?" she asked.

"Not just *any* witches," Suzanne explained. "We could go as Glinda the Good Witch and the Wicked Witch of the West from *The Wizard of Oz*."

Katie eyed her suspiciously. "And you'd be Glinda, right?" she asked.

"Of course," Suzanne said with a smile. "After all, I'm the one who has a glittery pink and white tutu. I got it from my grandmother last Christmas, remember?" Suzanne explained. "You don't have anything like that. You never even took a dance class."

Suzanne hadn't taken that many dance classes, either. She'd tried studying ballet back in second grade, but she'd only lasted a few weeks. Still, her grandmother kept

4

sending her things like tutus and ballet-slipper necklaces. That was the only reason Suzanne had that tutu, and Katie knew it.

"Besides, it'll be more fun to be the Wicked Witch of the West," Suzanne continued. "You could paint your face and arms all green. And you could wear a fake nose . . . one with a wart on it."

Katie considered that for a minute. It might be kind of fun to use some really gross green face paint for Halloween. She could wear her mother's black cape and carry a straw broom. "Okay," she agreed finally. "We'll go as witches. And maybe we could dress Heather up as a munchkin."

Suzanne shook her head crossly. She obviously had no desire to spend Halloween with her one-year-old sister. "My mother is going to take her trick-or-treating while we're in school," she told Katie.

"It was just an idea," Katie said.

"Besides, we don't need a munchkin,"

Suzanne continued. "You and I are definitely going to win the best costume prize at this year's Halloween parade!"

Chapter 2

Katie and Suzanne weren't the only ones who were talking about Halloween that morning. Everyone was buzzing with excitement about it. As the girls headed inside the school building they caught up with George Brennan and Kevin Camilleri.

"In my old neighborhood a lot of kids had two costumes," George told Kevin. "They would wear one costume in the afternoon to go trick-or-treating. Then they would switch costumes and go back to the same houses at night. That way they could get twice as much candy."

"Your old neighborhood sounds like fun,"

Kevin said.

George shrugged. "It was okay. But it's better here."

Katie smiled kindly at him. George had moved to Cherrydale last year, at the beginning of third grade. Before that, his family had moved around a lot. She knew he was happy to be in one place for a while.

"Well, I know where I *won't* be trick-or-treating this year," Kevin said. "That old house on Elm Lane."

Suzanne shuddered. "That place gives me the creeps. The wooden shingles are all rotting, and the chimney looks like it's going to fall off any minute."

"How about those spiderwebs in the windows?" George reminded her. "And I think there are rats in the yard."

"That house is awful," Katie agreed.

"I hear it's haunted!" Kevin exclaimed.

Suzanne shook her head. "There's no such thing as a real haunted house, Kevin! It's just an old abandoned house."

"It's *not* abandoned. Someone lives there," Kevin argued.

"No, they don't," Katie insisted, agreeing with Suzanne. "There hasn't been *anybody* in that old house for a long, long time. Not since the olden days, like when our *parents* were kids."

"You're right, no-*body* lives there," Kevin told her. "But ghosts do. I know it for sure."

"How?" Suzanne wanted to know.

"My big brother Ian was walking on Elm Lane last night, and he saw a light switch on and off," Kevin told the others. "If no one lives in the house, then how do you explain that?"

"Wow," George murmured. "That place really must be haunted."

Katie couldn't take it anymore. She hated thinking about ghosts and spiderwebs and rats. She walked toward the school building, leaving Suzanne, Kevin, and George behind.

As she headed off, she could hear her friends talking.

"What did you have to do that for?" she heard Suzanne asking Kevin. "You know how Katie gets when you talk about scary stuff."

"Yeah, she can be kind of a scaredy-cat," Kevin agreed. "I guess I forgot."

Katie frowned. Her friends might have thought she was too far ahead of them to hear what they were saying, but she could hear every word. And it made her very upset. She hated when they talked about her that way.

But how could Katie argue with them? When it came to ghosts, she *was* a scaredy-cat!

Chapter 3

"Welcome to the class 4A haunted mansion," Katie's teacher, Mr. Guthrie, greeted the class as they entered their classroom. "Home of Cherrydale's largest collection of ghosts and goblins."

Katie frowned. Even her teacher was getting into all this ghost stuff.

But as soon as she entered the room, Katie realized there was nothing to be afraid of in class 4A. Mr. Guthrie's ghosts weren't creepy or spooky. They were silly, happy cardboard ghosts with big smiles on their faces. They were hanging from the ceiling, taped to the walls, and pasted to the windows. A rubber skeleton was hanging from one of the light fixtures. There were goofy witches, too, with paper legs that had been folded back and forth like long black accordions. Even Slinky, the class snake, had gotten into the Halloween spirit. Mr. G. had placed a few fake spiderwebs around Slinky's glass cage. Katie bet no other classroom in all of Cherrydale Elementary School looked this cool.

"As soon as you come in, you can start decorating your beanbags," Mr. G. told the kids. He pointed to the far corner of the room. "I've got plenty of construction paper, fake spiders, cobwebs, and other materials for you to use."

Katie smiled. Decorating her beanbag was one of her favorite things to do in school. All of the kids in class 4A sat in beanbag chairs instead of at desks, because Mr. G. believed kids learned better when they were comfortable. Every few weeks the kids got to decorate their beanbag chairs in a new way.

DISCARD
NORMAL PUBLIC LIBRARY
NORMAL, ILLINOIS

Katie took a piece of black construction paper and began to cut out a triangle. She was going to turn her yellow beanbag into a big jack-o'-lantern. The triangle would be the jack-o'-lantern's nose.

"This is so much fun," Emma Weber said as she began taping black plastic spiders around the top of her beanbag chair. "I love Halloween."

"Me too," Katie told her. "I can't wait to trick-or-treat on Friday."

Emma W. sighed. "Lacey and I have to take Matthew and the twins with us when we get home from school in the afternoon," she said.

"Oh." Katie wasn't surprised by that. Emma and her older sister, Lacey, had to watch their three younger brothers a lot. Matthew was in first grade, so he wasn't a lot of trouble. But the twins, Timmy and Tyler, were tough. They were little toddlers who were just learning to walk. They were always getting into some kind of trouble. Emma was going to have her hands full with them—especially after they ate a lot of sugary candy.

"Well, maybe you can take your brothers in the afternoon and then come trick-or-treating with Suzanne, Jeremy, Kevin, George, and me after dinner," Katie suggested. "We're going to have lots of fun. My mom is going to take us. And she always dresses up, too."

Emma brightened. "That sounds like a great idea!" she exclaimed.

George taped a small plastic skeleton on his beanbag. "Do you guys know why the skeleton didn't cross the road?" he asked.

"Why not?" Andy Epstein wondered.

"Because he didn't have the guts!" George exclaimed.

The kids all laughed. All except Kadeem Carter, that is. Kadeem never laughed at George's jokes. He liked his own jokes better. "What do ghosts serve for dessert?" he asked the kids.

"What?" Mandy Banks wondered.

"Ice scream!" Kadeem shouted out, laughing.

"That's such an old joke," George told him. "Now here's a good one: What's a witch's favorite subject in school?"

"Spell-ing," Kadeem answered. "That joke is so old, the last time I heard it I fell off my dinosaur."

"Good one, Kadeem," Kevin laughed.

George glared at his best friend. "Traitor," he mumbled under his breath.

"What?" Kevin asked him. "It was funny."

"Not as funny as *this* joke," George assured him. "Why do witches fly on brooms?"

"Why?" Kevin asked.

"Because vacuum-cleaner cords aren't long enough," George told him with a laugh.

Kadeem opened his mouth to tell another joke, but Mr. G. spoke first. "Let's save the scary joke-off for Friday. That's Halloween, after all. On that day we can turn 4A into ghoul school!" He let out a silly-scary kind of laugh.

The kids all giggled.

"I wish every day could be Halloween!" Kadeem shouted out.

Katie gasped. That was the scariest thing she'd heard all day. Kadeem had made a wish. And wishes could be really scary—especially when they came true.

Chapter 4

Katie knew all about wishes coming true. It all started one horrible day back in third grade. On that day, Katie had lost the football game for her team. Then she'd splashed mud all over her favorite jeans. After that, George had made fun of her and called her a mud monster.

But the worst part of the day came when Katie had let out a loud burp—right in front of the whole class. It had been so embarrassing!

That night, Katie had made a wish to be anyone but herself. There must have been a shooting star overhead when she made the wish, because the very next day the magic wind came.

The magic wind was a really powerful tornado that blew only around Katie. It was so strong, it could blow her right out of her body . . . *and into someone else's*!

The first time the magic wind blew, it turned Katie into Speedy, the hamster in her third-grade class. Katie spent the whole morning going round and round on a hamster wheel and chewing on Speedy's wooden chew sticks. They didn't taste very good at all.

The magic wind came back again and again after that. Once it turned Katie into her cocker spaniel, Pepper. That had been *sooooo*

strange. Katie had gone to the bathroom on a fire hydrant, eaten a half-chewed bagel off the street, and gotten into a big fight with a nut-throwing squirrel.

And that was nothing compared to the time Katie turned into Suzanne, just as Suzanne was about to go onstage for her big modeling show. Somehow Katie had managed to put Suzanne's leather pants on backward. And she'd had a really tough time walking in those high-heeled shoes. A lot of the kids from school had been there to see Suzanne model. That meant they'd seen what a mess

Katie had made of things. When it was all over, Suzanne was really embarrassed—and confused. She had no idea that it hadn't been her up there on the runway. It had been Katie.

Something awful always happened when Katie switcherooed into someone else. Like the time the magic wind turned Katie into Emma W. That time, Katie had actually lost Timmy and Tyler. Emma could have gotten into big trouble if Katie hadn't found the boys just before the magic wind returned and switcherooed her back into herself.

That was why Katie didn't make wishes anymore. When they came true, they really made a mess of things.

Especially a wish like Kadeem's. As much as Katie loved Halloween, she didn't want Kadeem's wish to come true. She didn't want every day to be Halloween. Then the holiday wouldn't be special anymore.

Katie looked up at the big blackboard in the front of the room. Mr. G. was busy writing the date and the WFT—"Word for Today"—on the board.

MONDAY, OCTOBER 27
WFT: PETRIFY

Katie didn't have to wait for Mr. G. to write down the definition of that word. She already knew all about being petrified. That was exactly how she felt every time the magic wind came.

Chapter 5

"So what candy is your mom giving out this year for Halloween?" Suzanne asked Katie later that afternoon as the girls walked toward Katie's house. They were going to start planning their costumes.

"I'm not sure. I think she bought some bubble gum and those little chocolate bars," Katie replied.

"You're so lucky," Suzanne told her. "My mom gives out pencils. Hardly anyone comes to my house to trick-or-treat."

"Mew. Mew."

Just as the girls reached Katie's house, they noticed something moving in one of the bushes!

A little black kitten poked its head out from between the leaves and scampered quickly across a nearby lawn.

"Oh, look at that kitty," Katie cooed. "It's so tiny."

"Whose cat is it?" Suzanne asked.

"I don't know," Katie replied. "I've never seen it before." A look of concern crossed her face. "It's not wearing a collar. Do you think it could be a stray?"

"Who knows?" Suzanne replied. "Come on. Let's go inside. Maybe we can get your mom to take us to the mall right now. We've got to get going on those costumes."

"Suzanne, how can you think about costumes when that poor little kitty is probably all alone in the world? I'm going to get her some milk."

"No!" Suzanne shouted out.

"Why not?" Katie asked. "She looks hungry."

"Katie, you can't go anywhere near that

kitten," Suzanne insisted. "If you do, you'll ruin everything."

"What are you talking about?" Katie asked.

"That's a black cat," Suzanne explained. "Black cats are bad luck."

"Huh?"

Suzanne shook her head in disbelief. "Don't you know about black cats? If one crosses your path, you'll have bad luck. We'll probably lose the Halloween parade contest."

Katie sighed. "But—" she began.

"You have to stay away from that black cat," Suzanne insisted. She folded her arms across her chest. "Otherwise, we can't be partners anymore."

Katie frowned. It had been Suzanne's idea to be partners to begin with. Katie would have been just as happy being a cocker spaniel for Halloween. But she had already agreed to be the Wicked Witch of the West, and she couldn't go back on her promise.

"Okay, I'll stay away from the kitten," Katie

assured her friend.

"Good," Suzanne said. "Anyway, I'm sure the kitten's mother is somewhere. She'll take care of her."

Katie sighed as she heard the kitten mewing sadly from the side of the house. It sure didn't sound like her mother was nearby. It sounded like the kitten was lost and all alone.

"Now, about our costumes," Suzanne said, pulling Katie's attention away from the kitten. "Like I said, I'm going to wear my fancy tutu. And I thought I would go to the mall and buy a glittery magic wand and matching crown."

"Cool," Katie said. "You'll look really pretty."

"I know," Suzanne agreed. "Now we need to make *you* look really *scary*. We'll have to get a really tall black witch hat and one of those witch costumes. You know, the kind that comes in a bag. They usually have a dress and a cape in them."

"Oh, I'm not going to buy my costume," Katie told her. "I'm going to make it, like I do every year."

"But Katie, this isn't every year. This year we're going to win the Halloween contest at school," Suzanne insisted. "And it isn't going to be easy. I overheard Jeremy Fox telling Manny Gonzalez and Sam McDonough that he was building a robot costume out of real metal!"

"Wow!" Katie exclaimed. "Jeremy always has the best costumes."

"His aunt helps him, that's why," Suzanne said knowingly. "She designs costumes for plays in New York. My mother told me. So, if we're going to beat him, you'd better *buy* your witch dress."

"No way," Katie insisted. "Don't worry. My mom and I will make something really cool. We'll go to the fabric store at the mall tonight and pick out some really creepy black cloth."

"All right, as long as you're sure it will be scary," Suzanne agreed.

"I promise," Katie vowed.

"Maybe I should come along," Suzanne continued. "Just so I can see if the costume is good enough."

Katie sighed. Suzanne was so bossy sometimes. But there was no point in arguing with her. She was going to come anyway.

"Whatever you want," Katie told her friend. She tried to sound excited about shopping. But the truth was, all she could think about was that poor little kitty.

Chapter 6

"Hey, there's Jeremy!" Katie shouted as she walked into the Fun and Funky Fabric Store in the Cherrydale Mall. She hurried over to where Jeremy Fox was standing. Katie's mother and Suzanne followed close behind her.

"Hi, Katie. Hello, Mrs. Carew," Jeremy greeted Katie and her mom. "Hi, Suzanne," he added less enthusiastically.

Just then a tall dark-haired woman with glasses just like Jeremy's came walking over. "Jeremy, I found the perfect silver-colored cloth . . ." She stopped when she noticed the girls. "Oh, hi," she greeted them sweetly.

"You guys know my Aunt Sheila," Jeremy said.

"Well, my mom and I do," Katie told him. "But I don't think Suzanne has met her."

"I'm Suzanne Lock," Suzanne introduced herself. "I've heard all about you. You design costumes for shows. That's interesting to me, because I am an actress."

"An actress. Yeah, right," Jeremy snorted. "What show have you ever been in?"

Suzanne frowned. "Well, I am going to be an actress. Right now, I'm modeling."

"You're taking modeling classes," Jeremy corrected her. "It's not the same thing."

"Well, I'm happy to meet you, Suzanne," Jeremy's aunt said. "Jeremy and I are just picking out some of the materials for his robot costume. I came into town to help him. I just adore Halloween!"

"Me too!" Katie squealed.

"Who doesn't?" Suzanne said. She smiled at Jeremy's Aunt Sheila. "It's so theatrical!"

Jeremy rolled his eyes. "Oh, no. She's acting like Suzanne Superstar again."

Katie giggled. Suzanne had decided that when she became famous, her name was going to be Suzanne Superstar. The kids thought that was ridiculous.

"My costume is going to be so cool," Jeremy said. "Aunt Sheila is going to use all these soda cans and silver fabric to make me look like a real robot."

"That sounds fantastic!" Katie told him.

"I can't wait to see you when you come to our house to trick-or-treat," Mrs. Carew added.

"I think I have a real chance of winning the prize at the parade this year," Jeremy continued.

"Nice try," Suzanne interrupted. "But Katie and I are going to win this year."

"What are you guys going as?" Jeremy asked the girls.

Katie opened her mouth to speak, but Suzanne stopped her. "It's a secret," Suzanne told Jeremy. "No one can know but Katie and me."

"What's the big deal?" Jeremy asked her. "It's not like I'm going to change my costume and copy you or anything."

"Well, I can tell you what Pepper's going to be for Halloween this year," Katie said, trying to change the subject. "I got him a clown hat. But I don't think he'll wear it for very long. Pepper hates hats."

Jeremy laughed. "Remember what he did to those antlers you put on him last Christmas?"

"Uh-huh," Katie recalled, giggling. "He shredded them! But he had a lot of fun doing it!"

"Pepper's funny," Jeremy said with a chuckle. "You are so lucky to have a pet."

Katie knew how badly he wanted to have a pet of his own. But his mom didn't really want an animal in the house. She thought they were too messy.

"I remember how much your mom and I wanted a pet when we were kids," Jeremy's Aunt Sheila recalled.

Jeremy looked surprised. "My mother wanted a pet?" he asked her.

"Oh, yes," his aunt said. "In fact, she and I used to feed all the stray cats and dogs in the neighborhood. We would leave bits of food behind our house for them so they wouldn't starve."

Katie frowned. Hearing about that made

her remember the little black kitten. She hoped it wasn't starving right now. Katie felt kind of awful about listening to Suzanne. Maybe she should have helped the kitten, instead.

"I'm surprised your mom hasn't gotten a pet by now," Jeremy's aunt continued. "She used to love animals a lot."

"No way!" Jeremy exclaimed.

His Aunt Sheila laughed. "Way," she replied. "Keep working on her, Jeremy. And I'll talk to her, too. Maybe between us we can get her to remember how much she always wanted a pet."

"That would be awesome!" Jeremy said hopefully.

"It sure would," Katie agreed.

"Are we going to stand here and talk about animals all night?" Suzanne asked Katie. "We have costumes to put together, remember?"

Katie sighed. Suzanne hated it when the conversation was about something other than what she was interested in. But this time she was probably right. It was getting late, and Katie still hadn't bought her witch hat or the black fabric for her costume. "Yeah, we'd better go look for that black—" she began.

"Ahem," Suzanne cleared her throat. It was a signal for Katie to stop talking. "It's a secret, remember?"

"I think what you need is in the back of the store, Katie," Mrs. Carew suggested. "Let's check there. It was nice seeing you, Sheila. Good luck with your costume, Jeremy."

"And good luck with the pet," Katie told Jeremy as she walked away.

Chapter 7

"Pepper, don't you want to walk outside with me?" Katie asked her dog early Tuesday morning. Usually the cocker spaniel liked to walk Katie to the end of the block. But today Pepper snorted a little and buried his head in his front paws.

"Guess you don't want to go out in the rain," Katie said as she walked out onto her front lawn and opened up her umbrella. It was Katie's favorite umbrella—the green one with the big frog eyes on top.

The rain was coming down hard, and the umbrella wasn't really helping very much. Katie walked as fast as she could. She wanted

to get to school really quickly. Otherwise, she'd spend the whole day in wet clothes.

"*Mew. Mew.*"

Katie turned around and saw the little black kitten standing under a tree. It looked like the kitten was trying to find a dry place to stand. But the rain was falling hard now, and the leaves weren't keeping the cat very dry.

"Poor little kitty," Katie said.

The stray cat looked up at Katie, and then dashed off down the block in the opposite direction.

"Phew, that was close," Katie sighed. She was glad the black cat hadn't crossed her path. Now she didn't have to worry about bad luck. But the kitten sure did. It was *really* bad luck to be stuck out in the rain with nothing to eat.

"Hey, Suzanne," George called out that afternoon during lunch. "Are you gonna eat your chocolate pudding?"

Suzanne was sitting next to Katie at the lunch table. The girls both looked up and glanced across the table at George's lunch tray. He had mixed in his chocolate pudding with his spaghetti and meat sauce and creamed spinach. Then he had poured in some of his fruit punch and stirred it all together.

"Not anymore," Suzanne said, making a face as she pushed the small cup of pudding toward George.

"Thanks!" he exclaimed as he poured the pudding over the rest of the mess.

"Oh, George, that is the grossest thing I've ever seen," Miriam Chan groaned.

"This cafeteria is getting disgusting," Mandy Banks agreed.

"Here, George, add this," Kevin said, dumping part of his jelly sandwich onto George's tray.

George grinned and rolled the bread and jelly into a bunch of little balls, which he placed all around the mushy mountain of food.

"Hey, Kev, do you know what made the jelly roll?" George asked him.

"No, what?"

"It saw the apple turnover." George began to laugh hysterically.

Suzanne rolled her eyes. "Not funny, George," she told him.

"*I* think it's funny," Kevin said.

"Me too," Jeremy agreed. "Got any more good ones today, George?"

"Sure, I got a million of 'em," George assured him. "Did you ever hear the story of oatmeal?"

"Nope," Jeremy answered.

"Ah, never mind," George said. "It's just a lot of mush!"

The boys all started laughing again. George looked back over at Katie's tray. "Are you going to finish your cream cheese sandwich?" he asked her.

Katie began to hand George the other half of her cream cheese sandwich. Then she stopped herself. "Uh, I'm going to eat it," she told him. "Just not now." She wrapped the half of the sandwich in her napkin and held on to it.

"What are you going to do with that?" Suzanne asked her.

"I'm saving it for later. In case I get hungry during class," Katie told her.

"You can't eat in class," Suzanne said.

"Well, then I'll eat it after school," Katie told her. "On my way home. Sometimes I get hungry."

Suzanne looked at her curiously but said nothing. She just went back to eating her own lunch.

Katie frowned. She hated lying. Especially to one of her best friends. But she couldn't tell Suzanne what she really planned to do with the sandwich. It would make her too angry.

Chapter 8

"Hey Katie, do you want to come over to my house?" Jeremy asked as they left school that afternoon. "The rain's stopped, so we can play in my yard. And I just got a new soccer ball."

Katie shook her head. "Sorry. I've got something to do today."

Suzanne strutted over and put her arm around Katie's shoulder. "That's right. Katie and I still have some finishing touches to put on our costumes."

"Actually, I can't do that, either," Katie told her.

"But Katie, it's already Tuesday and—"

44

X

Suzanne began.

"I'm sorry, Suzanne. I can't today," Katie repeated. "But don't worry. My mom and I have the whole thing under control."

"Okay," Suzanne told her. But she didn't sound very sure.

"So, what are you doing this afternoon, anyway?" Jeremy asked her.

"Nothing. Just an errand," Katie told him. "Oh, well, I gotta go." And with that, Katie ran off, leaving Jeremy and Suzanne behind.

× × ×

"Here, kitty, kitty. Here, kitty, kitty," Katie called out as soon as she was a few blocks from school. As she walked, she felt around inside the pocket of her Windbreaker. Good. The cream cheese sandwich was still there.

Katie hoped the little black kitten would like the sandwich. Katie wasn't really sure what kittens ate. But she figured that cream cheese was made from milk, and cats liked milk, so . . .

"Mew. Mew."

Katie looked up. There on the lower branches of a tree was the kitten!

"Here, kitty, kitty," Katie called as she slowly walked over to the tree. She held up the sandwich half. "I brought you something."

The cat stood very, very still, trying to disappear in the leaves of the tree. But Katie could still see her. She reached up her hand. "See, it's yummy. I'm sorry I didn't feed you before, but now . . ."

Before Katie could finish her sentence, the kitten leaped out of the tree and scurried across a nearby fence.

"Don't be afraid, little kitten," Katie called as the cat jumped onto the sidewalk.

The kitten sure was fast. Its black paws padded speedily along the ground. Katie followed close behind. She really wanted to make sure the little cat had a good meal.

Katie was watching the cat so carefully that she didn't even realize where she was going. Before she knew it, Katie was on Elm Lane.

Katie gasped as she watched the cat turn off from the sidewalk and make its way over to an old house with a crooked chimney, rotting shingles, and dead rosebushes.

Katie knew what house this was.

The cat had gone right to the haunted house Kevin had warned the kids about yesterday! Oh, no!

The kitten stood perfectly still at the side of the house, next to an old rusty railing. The window nearest the cat was slightly cracked, and a spider had begun to spin its web in the corner.

Katie really wanted to run away! But she knew she couldn't do that. She had to save the kitten. She had to get to it before the ghosts inside captured it.

Just then, a light went on in one of the upstairs windows. Katie gulped. That was just like what Kevin's big brother, Ian, had seen. The kitten had awakened the ghosts. And now they were coming after her!

At that very moment, a woman with a pointy chin, a long nose, and wild black and gray hair stuck her head out of the window. "Scat, you cat!" she shouted in an old, crackly voice.

Katie was so scared, she could barely breathe. Ian Camilleri had been wrong. Ghosts weren't the scariest things inside the haunted house. There was something far worse in there.

There was a witch living in the haunted house on Elm Lane.

"AAHHHH!" Katie shouted out. She dropped the sandwich in fear.

The kitten lifted its head and looked around. Then, suddenly, the black cat darted across the yard and ran off . . . *crossing right in front of Katie's path.*

Oh, that was bad. Really bad. But Katie didn't have time to think about it now. She turned and ran toward home. She had to get out of there before the Witch of Elm Lane spotted her!

Chapter 9

"Kevin, you were right!" Katie shouted as she raced toward Kevin, George, and Jeremy on the playground the next morning. "That old house *is* haunted."

"I told you. Ian saw the ghosts," Kevin told her.

Katie shook her head excitedly. "No, it's haunted by a *witch*. She lives there, and I saw her!" Katie's voice started to shake when she thought about the pointy-faced, gray-haired woman. "She was so scary."

"No way!" Kevin gasped. "You went to the haunted house?"

Suddenly, the kids who were busy playing

nearby stopped what they were doing and circled around Katie.

All but Suzanne, that is. Katie watched as her best friend turned away, pretending to look in her backpack for something. Suzanne was obviously angry that—for once—she wasn't the center of attention.

But Katie didn't care. This was huge. And she wanted everyone to know about it!

"Yeah," Katie continued. "I went to the house. Yesterday, after school."

"Whoa, Katie Kazoo, that totally rocks!" George cheered.

"But that place is so scary," Jeremy said, sounding amazed. "And you're usually such a . . ." He stopped himself before he could say something that might hurt Katie's feelings.

"A scaredy-cat?" Katie finished his sentence. She smiled at the surprised look on Jeremy's face. He didn't realize that she had heard her friends call her that. "Well, I guess I'm not, huh?"

"No way," Miriam Chan told her. "Not if you went to Elm Lane alone."

"I did," Katie assured her. "All by myself. And I saw the witch in person."

Now the crowd around Katie was getting bigger and bigger. It seemed like everyone— even some fifth-graders—wanted to hear her story.

"She poked her head outside of a window while I was there," Katie continued. "And she yelled really loudly." Katie shivered. "The Witch of Elm Lane has a voice that is all crackly and very creepy!"

Miriam shivered. "The Witch of Elm Lane," she repeated. "That sounds so scary."

"She *is* scary," Katie assured.

"What did the witch look like?" a fifth-grade girl named Rachel asked her.

"She has wild black and gray hair with cobwebs in it," Katie told her. "Her chin's pointy, her nose is long, and her face is covered with witch dust!"

"Whoa," Rachel said with a shiver. "She sounds awful."

"Oh, she is," Katie assured her.

"You must have been really scared, Katie," Zoe Canter said.

Katie nodded. "I was. But not as scared as the black cat in her yard," she told her. "That kitten ran away so fast when the witch screamed that I couldn't even see her paws moving. It was just a big blur."

"Wow! You went near a witch *and* a black cat! You are really brave," Isobel, another fifth-grader, said, complimenting her.

Katie smiled proudly. No one had ever called her brave before. But now a *fifth*-grader had. She could hardly believe it.

Katie hadn't felt very brave yesterday afternoon. And she certainly hadn't gone to Elm Lane on purpose. She had just been trying to take care of the stray kitten.

But the other kids didn't know that. And Katie wasn't going to tell them. She wanted them to think she'd just been really brave and gone to the house on purpose.

So she told them a part of the story that she knew would impress them even more.

"And that's not all," Katie continued, standing tall. "While I was near the haunted house, that black cat ran right in front of me!"

"I can't believe you, Katie!" Suzanne shouted out suddenly.

Katie looked surprised. Suzanne had been listening to her story, after all.

"You let that black cat cross your path. Now you're going to have bad luck!" Suzanne said with a scowl.

"Gosh, Suzanne, why are you getting so upset about it?" Jeremy asked. "It's not *your* problem."

"Yes, it is!" Suzanne told him. "Katie's my partner in the Halloween parade. And now we're going to lose the contest!"

"Come on, Suzanne, you're being silly,"

Emma W. told her. "Black cats don't really bring bad luck. That's just a silly superstition."

Suzanne didn't think so. "I am never going to forgive you for this, Katie. In fact, I'm not even talking to you!" she said as she stormed away angrily.

Katie frowned as Suzanne walked away. She hadn't meant to upset Suzanne. She had just wanted to give the kitten some food. But now Suzanne was really mad at her. Katie hated when her friends were angry. Maybe the cat had been bad luck, after all.

"*I* think that cat brought you good luck," Jeremy said, interrupting Katie's thoughts. "I've been trying to get Suzanne to stop talking for years!"

Katie sighed. Suddenly, having the other kids think she was brave didn't seem all that important. She just wanted Suzanne to stop being mad at her. Katie started to walk toward Suzanne so she could apologize. But a fifth-grader named Benjamin stopped her.

"I can't believe a *fourth*-grader would be brave enough to do all that," he told Katie. "I think you're lying."

The other fifth-graders nodded in agreement.

"No, I'm not," Katie insisted. "I really did see the witch."

"Prove it," Benjamin demanded. "Go back there today after school. I'll come with you. I want to see this witch."

"Me too," Rachel said.

"That *would* be kind of cool, Katie Kazoo," George added.

"I really want to go, too," Kevin said. "My brother would be really impressed if I saw a witch. Even *he's* never seen one of those."

Katie really didn't want to go back to the house on Elm Lane. But she knew she had to. Otherwise, the kids would all think she was lying.

And they would call her a scaredy-cat again. Especially Suzanne. She was really

mad at Katie. She'd be glad to be able to say
something mean about her.

Katie really didn't want that to happen.

"Okay," she told the kids. "Meet me here
after school. I'll take you there this
afternoon."

Chapter 10

"Okay, Katie, let's see if you really are
brave enough to talk to a witch," Benjamin
dared Katie later that afternoon. He had been
walking right beside her ever since they'd left
school. There was no way he was letting her
chicken out of going to the haunted house.

Now there was a whole crowd of fourth-
and fifth-graders walking behind them.

"I . . . uh . . . I didn't say I'd talk to her,"
Katie insisted. "I don't even know if she'll be
home."

"Of course she will," Benjamin insisted.
"Witches don't go out during the daytime."

"That's vampires," George said, correcting

him. He rolled his eyes. "Sheesh. Everyone knows that."

"We're almost there," Isobel noted excitedly as the group of kids turned the corner. "Elm Lane's the next block."

Katie walked a few more feet. Then the crooked chimney came into view. The kids could see it over the old trees with the dead leaves.

Katie gulped. The house was scarier than she had remembered.

CRASH!

The group heard the sound of breaking glass coming from one of the cobweb-covered windows. Katie's heart started to pound wildly. The witch *was* home. And she sounded mad.

"Oh, man, I just realized my mom wanted me home early," Rachel said.

"Yeah, look at the time," Isobel agreed, looking at her wrist.

"How do you know what time it is?" George

asked her. "You don't even have a watch on."

Isobel didn't answer him. Instead, she called out, "Wait up, Rachel," as she raced to catch up with her friend.

"What wimps," Kevin shouted, loudly enough for the fifth-grade girls to hear him.

Just then, a whole flock of geese flew from the roof of the house. Their wild honking grew louder and louder as they passed overhead. They seemed to cover the whole sky as they zoomed away.

"Those birds sure look scared," Kadeem gulped. "If that place is too creepy for them, it's too creepy for me."

"You're not kidding," Manny agreed. "I don't need to see any witch. I believe you, Katie."

"Um . . . Katie," Jeremy said, "you know, this took a little longer than I thought it would. I gotta get to soccer practice." He started to head back toward his house.

Katie turned to him and frowned. Some

best friend he was.

"Well, if Jeremy's leaving, I'm going, too," Becky Stern said. She hurried to catch up to Jeremy.

$$\times \quad \times \quad \times$$

Soon the only people left were Katie, Kevin, George, and Benjamin.

"Okay, Katie, prove to us that there really is a witch living there," Benjamin said. "Ring the doorbell."

"Yeah, go ahead, Katie," Kevin urged. "I want to tell Ian that I saw a real witch."

Katie stood there for a moment, staring at the big cobweb-covered house. She did not want to go up those steps. She wanted to run away as fast as she could!

"Come on, Katie," Benjamin insisted. "Do it . . . *unless you're scared.*"

"I . . . I . . . I'm not scared," Katie stammered, sounding very scared indeed.

"Then go ahead," Benjamin said.

Slowly, Katie walked up the rickety old

wooden stairs that led to the front porch. She could hear the squeaking under her feet. There was a big black spider spinning a web on the banister.

"Eeek!!" Katie jumped up with surprise as a rat scampered into the bushes near the porch.

"I'm out of here!" Kevin shouted at the sound of Katie's scream.

"Right behind you, buddy," George added, running off.

Benjamin didn't say a word. He just took off.

Oh, no! This was *too* creepy. There was no way Katie was going to ring that doorbell. She didn't care if the kids called her a scaredy-cat for the rest of her life!

"Hey, wait for me!" Katie cried out. She didn't want to be left there all alone.

But before Katie could run after the boys, she felt a cool breeze blowing on the back of her neck. She pulled her jacket tighter around her, but she could still feel a slight draft.

And then the breeze began to get really strong. Katie looked at the trees. Their leaves weren't moving. The grass wasn't blowing, either. In fact, the wind didn't seem to be blowing anywhere—except around Katie. Which could only mean one thing.

The magic wind was back!

The magic wind grew stronger and stronger, whirling around Katie so powerfully that she thought it would blow her away. She closed her eyes and tried not to cry.

And then it stopped. Just like that.

The magic wind was gone. And so was Katie.

She'd turned into someone else.

But who?

Chapter 11

"AHHHHHHH!" Katie screamed the loudest she ever had. When she opened her eyes, she found herself standing in front of a cracked mirror. The face that stared back at her had a long chin, a pointed nose, and gray and black hair with cobwebs hanging from it.

Oh, no! The magic wind had turned Katie into the Witch of Elm Lane!

"AAAAAAHHHHHHHHHHHHHH!" she screamed again.

Bong. Bong. Bong. Bong.

Clang. Clang. Clang. Clang.

Cuckoo. Cuckoo. Cuckoo. Cuckoo.

Suddenly, a bunch of really odd noises

began ringing throughout the old house. Katie jumped. Her hands started to shake. Ghosts! The house was filled with ghosts! And they were coming to get her!

Katie turned and looked for a place to hide. Maybe under the table, where that little glass clock was. Or maybe behind the big grandfather clock in the corner. Or under the big green sofa next to the cuckoo clock.

Boy, there sure are a lot of clocks in here, Katie thought. *They're everywhere.*

And that's when she realized what was happening. There weren't any ghosts in the house. All those noises were coming from the clocks. It was four o'clock, and they were all ringing at once.

Katie sat down in a wooden rocking chair and tried to catch her breath. She looked around the room for a minute.

It was strange, but the house didn't look nearly as scary from the inside as it did from the outside. Sure, it was really dirty, with dust and cobwebs everywhere. But there were nice things inside, too. Like the big, cushiony green velvet couch across the room.

And there was a beautiful stone sculpture of children playing in the corner of the room.

Overhead, a huge crystal chandelier hung from the ceiling. Even though it was covered with dust, Katie thought it was beautiful—like something you would see in a giant mansion.

Actually, the haunted house on Elm Lane really wasn't that scary after all.

Slowly, Katie stood up and began to look around. On the table in the hallway, she found another clock. This one was gold-colored. It sat inside a shiny glass dome.

The kitchen was just down the hall. Katie gulped as she walked into the room. There, on the stove, was a huge black pot.

The witch's cauldron! Katie sure hoped there wasn't any horrible potion cooking in there. Slowly, she walked over and peered inside the pot. Phew! It was empty.

Katie plopped down on one of the rickety wooden chairs and looked around the kitchen. It sure was old and dirty. The blood-red paint on the walls was chipping, and the ceiling had cracks in it. Still, someone had put up new red-and-white-checked curtains, and there were fresh flowers on the windowsill.

"That's weird," Katie muttered to herself. "What kind of a witch puts up curtains?"

Then, suddenly, something on the kitchen counter caught her eye. Three bright orange pumpkins were lined up in a row. Each one had been carefully carved into a jack-o'-lantern. But not just any old jack-o'-lanterns. *These* pumpkins were amazing! One had a cat carved into it. Another had a ghost shape. The third pumpkin was only half-carved. Katie wasn't sure what it was going to be. She moved a little closer to get a better look. Maybe she could guess . . .

CRASH!

Oh, no! As Katie turned around, her rear

end knocked over a silver clock that had been sitting on the counter. The glass that covered the face of the clock broke into about a hundred pieces.

I've got to clean this up, Katie thought. *If the witch finds out I've broken her clock, she's going to be really mad at me!*

Quickly, she searched for something to clean up the mess. She spotted an old straw broom with a wooden handle. It was leaning against a wall in the corner of the room.

Katie looked at the broom for a minute, not sure of what to do. Was that a regular broom? Or was that a magical witch's broom? Should she touch it? Would she start flying if she did?

"Wait a minute! I'm a witch now," Katie said to herself. "Maybe I can just put a spell on the broom and it will do all the cleaning up by itself."

There was only one problem: Katie didn't know any witch spells.

"Maybe I can make one up," Katie decided. She thought for a moment. Then she chanted, "Wood and straw make a broom. Now sweep up the glass in this room."

Katie stared at the broom. It didn't move. If Katie was going to clean the room, she was obviously going to have to do it the normal way.

She reached over and gently touched the broom. The wood felt smooth, just like the wood on her broom at home.

Katie wrapped both of her hands around the handle. Her feet stayed on the floor, and she didn't start flying around the room. That was a good sign.

Slowly, she began to sweep up the broken glass. With each movement of her hand, the glass moved across the floor into a neat little pile.

Phew. It was definitely just a regular, everyday broom.

In a few moments, Katie had cleaned up all of the shattered glass. She glanced over at the broken clock. It had been really pretty. But now it was kind of dented, and there was no glass to cover the hands. Katie had ruined the clock. She felt terrible about that.

There had to be some way she could make up for breaking the clock. But what?

Katie thought about the curtains and the flowers. Was it possible the witch had been trying to clean up around here? Did witches even do things like that?

Maybe. Katie didn't really know a whole lot about witches, actually. And if the witch was trying to make her house prettier, Katie could definitely help her out with that.

She grabbed the broom and went out to sweep up some of the dirt in the hallway.

Achoo! Katie sneezed as dust flew up all around her. "This place is really gross," she murmured.

She looked up and noticed a cobweb on the ceiling. Katie lifted up the broom and tried to knock the web to the floor. But instead of landing on the floor, the strands of sticky dust landed in Katie's hair.

"Ooh, yuck!" Katie cried out. She reached up and tried to yank it out. But the sticky threads were stuck in her wild gray and black hair.

Katie was very, very upset. She didn't want to be in this creepy old house anymore. She didn't want to have dust up her nose or cobwebs in her hair. And she *certainly* didn't

74

want to be a witch.

Katie sat down on the big green couch and began to cry. This was the worst day ever! The magic wind had switcherooed her into a lot of weird things before, but it had never changed her into anything as horrible as this!

Chapter 12

"Let Katie go!"

"Free our friend, you old witch!"

"Please don't eat Katie!"

Katie heard voices coming from the street outside the house. She peeked outside the window to see where they were coming from.

Wow! George, Kevin, and Benjamin were standing across the street, shouting. They had come back for her!

"There she is!" Kevin shouted nervously. "The witch!"

"Come on, let Katie go," George shouted to Katie.

"Don't eat our friend," Kevin added.

"She won't taste very good," Benjamin said. "She's just a scrawny fourth-grader."

Hey! Who is he calling scrawny? Katie thought angrily.

But she didn't stay angry for very long. She was too happy to see her friends again. She was so tired of being all alone in the creepy house.

Katie was so excited to see George, Kevin, and Benjamin that she forgot all about being turned into the Witch of Elm Lane.

She ran out onto the front porch. "It's okay!" she shouted to her pals. "I'm fine. Come on inside."

But George, Kevin, and Benjamin didn't see a fourth-grade girl on that porch. All they saw was an old lady with dust on her face, cobwebs in her hair, and a broom in her hand.

"AAAAAAHHHHHHHHHHHH! It's the witch!" the boys screamed as they ran off down the block.

Now Katie was all alone again. She sat

down on the steps and rested her head in her hands.

A cool breeze began nipping at the back of Katie's neck. She lifted up her head and looked around. The leaves in the trees were not moving. The spider was calmly spinning its web, and the dead leaves on the lawn were lying still.

The wind was only blowing on Katie. She knew what that meant.

The magic wind was back!

Within seconds, the magic wind began swirling around and around Katie, blowing harder and harder with each spin. Katie held onto the banister beside the stairs to keep from being blown away.

And then it stopped. Just like that.

The magic wind was gone.

Katie Carew was back. And so was the Witch of Elm Lane. In fact, she was sitting on the porch, *right next to Katie.*

This was *so* not good!

Chapter 13

"AAHHH!" Katie shouted, leaping to her feet.

"AAHHH!" the witch shouted, leaping to *her* feet. "What are you doing here?"

Katie didn't stop to give her an answer. She darted down the stairs. But the witch called after her.

"Stop. Wait. You don't have to go. I didn't mean to scream. I was just surprised to see you," the Witch of Elm Lane said, apologizing. She looked around. "Come to think of it, I'm kind of surprised to be out here. The last thing I remember, I was inside, carving pumpkins for Halloween."

Katie stopped. The witch didn't sound so scary after all. She just sounded like a normal old lady. A *very confused* normal old lady.

"I . . . um . . . think you came outside when you heard some of my friends shouting," Katie told her.

"Yes, I remember that. At least I think I do. It's all kind of fuzzy," the woman told her. "I remember you, though."

Katie gulped. "You do?"

"Yes. Aren't you the little girl who was here with a cat yesterday afternoon?"

Katie nodded. "It was a stray kitten. I was trying to feed her. But you scared her away."

"I know," the woman said. "I didn't want to. It's just that I had put some plant fertilizer around my rosebushes, and I was afraid if the kitten licked it, it might get sick. And the last thing I would want to do is hurt a little kitty."

"Oh, so you weren't being mean to the cat?" Katie asked, surprised.

"Of course not. Why would I be?" the woman

replied. "I love cats. I wish I could have one. But I do a lot of traveling. I love seeing different countries. And a cat needs someone around to keep it company."

"I *love* to travel," Katie told her. "During my last vacation I went to England, Spain, France, and Italy. My dog stayed with our next-door neighbors. He missed us a lot, I think."

"I'm sure he did," the woman said. "I go on *a lot* of vacations. Imagine how much a cat would miss me if I was gone from home for a long time."

"Is this your home?" Katie asked. "I didn't think anyone lived here."

"No one has, not for a long time," the woman replied. "But the house has been in my family for years. I decided to come and fix the place up and maybe live here, at least for a while." She stuck out her hand. "So I guess we're neighbors now. My name is Maggie Hamilton."

"I'm Katie Carew," Katie told her. "I live a few blocks away."

"It's very nice to meet you, Katie," Mrs. Hamilton said. "It's wonderful to have some company. I've been here a month now, and I haven't met anyone. Hardly anyone even walks by."

"That's because we thought the house was haunt—" Katie stopped herself before she could finish her sentence. She didn't want to hurt Mrs. Hamilton's feelings. "I mean . . . well, we didn't think anyone lived here. And then when I saw you yell at the cat . . ."

Mrs. Hamilton laughed. "I must have looked awful that day. I had dust on my face, and a few cobwebs had fallen on me. You must have thought I was a witch or something." She laughed again.

Katie blushed but didn't answer.

Mrs. Hamilton grinned. "And I probably don't look much better now. I'm sorry to be so untidy. I've been cleaning all day. You

wouldn't believe what a mess it is in there."
She looked down at her dust-covered dress.
"Or maybe you would."

Oh, Katie would believe it. She'd seen the
mess, after all. But she couldn't tell Mrs.
Hamilton that. Then she'd have to explain all
about the magic wind.

"I guess I'll meet most of the local children
on Halloween. I plan on buying lots of candy
to give out when they come trick-or-treating,"
Mrs. Hamilton told Katie. She smiled warmly.
"I just love Halloween. My favorite thing
to do is carve jack-o'-lanterns. I can carve
almost any shape into a pumpkin. I can't wait
for you and your friends to see them!"

Katie frowned. She knew none of the kids
would be coming to visit Mrs. Hamilton on
Halloween—not since Katie told them that
Mrs. Hamilton was a witch.

But Mrs. Hamilton wasn't a witch at all.
She was just a nice, lonely old lady who was
cleaning up her house.

"Would you like to come inside and see my jack-o'-lanterns now?" Mrs. Hamilton asked her. "I'm working on a special one at the moment—it's going to be a skeleton!"

"Well, I . . ." Katie began. Then suddenly she heard a loud bong and some ringing coming from inside the house. The clocks were chiming. "What time is it?" she asked Mrs. Hamilton.

"It must be four thirty," Mrs. Hamilton told her. "My clocks all ring once on the half-hour."

"Four thirty? Oh, no! I'm late for my cooking class!" Katie exclaimed. She couldn't believe she had forgotten that it was Wednesday. She was supposed to have been at the Cherrydale Community Center fifteen minutes ago. "We're making pumpkin pie today."

"Mmm . . . my favorite," Mrs. Hamilton said. "You'd better get going. It was nice meeting you, Katie. I hope I will see you and your friends on Halloween."

"You will," Katie assured her, trying hard to smile. "I'll make sure they're here."

But as she ran down the path, Katie sighed. She had absolutely no idea how she was going to do that. Convincing the kids at school that there was no Witch of Elm Lane wasn't going to be easy. Not at all.

Chapter 14

"Katie Kazoo! Am I glad to see you!" George exclaimed the next morning as Katie walked onto the playground.

"I'll say," Emma W. agreed, hurrying over to Katie. "George and Kevin told me that the Witch of Elm Lane had captured you and eaten you for supper."

Katie looked over at George. "Why did you tell her that?" she asked him.

"Well, when we didn't see you outside the witch's house, Kevin, Benjamin, and I just thought—" George began.

"Well, you thought wrong," Katie told him. "I'm fine. And if you were so worried, why didn't you call me later?"

George looked down at the ground. "I don't know. We didn't think of it, I guess. We were just so freaked out. I mean, there was the witch, and that unlucky cat, and . . ."

"Black cats don't bring bad luck," Katie insisted. "And there is no Witch of Elm Lane."

"Yes, there is," George insisted. "I saw her. And so did Kevin and Benjamin. She came out onto her porch and yelled at us."

By now, a whole crowd of kids had gathered around. It seemed to Katie that George and Kevin must have told everyone in the whole school about what had happened—or what they *thought* had happened—yesterday afternoon.

"Well, at least you and I can be partners in the Halloween parade again," Suzanne told Katie.

Katie looked at her curiously. "You're not mad at me anymore?"

Suzanne shook her head. "Of course not.

89

You've already had your bad luck. You got stuck in that haunted house with the witch!"

"I told you. She's not a—" Katie began.

But Benjamin interrupted her. "She was the scariest witch I've ever seen," he boasted to the other kids.

Katie rolled her eyes. "How many witches have you seen, Benjamin?" she asked him.

"You know what I mean," Benjamin told her. "When she came out onto her porch, she even had her broomstick with her."

"How did you manage to escape from the witch's house, Katie?" Isobel asked her. "You must have been really scared in there."

For a moment, Katie thought about bragging about making a great escape from the clutches of an evil witch. After all, the kids did think she was really brave and everything.

But she couldn't do that. It wouldn't be fair to Mrs. Hamilton. She was such a nice old lady. Katie didn't want the kids to be frightened of her anymore.

"There's nothing to be scared of," Katie told Isobel. "There's no witch in that house."

"Then who did George, Benjamin, and Kevin see?" Isobel asked her.

"That's Mrs. Hamilton. She lives there," Katie told her.

"Nobody lives there . . . except the witch," Kevin insisted.

"Mrs. Hamilton just moved in. She's trying to clean the house up. That's why she was carrying a broom when you saw her," Katie explained to Benjamin. "And she's not a witch. She's just a nice old lady."

"It looked like a witch's broom," Kevin insisted.

"Well, it's not," Katie told him. "It's just a broom. And Mrs. Hamilton is really great. She collects clocks. Really cool ones. And you should see the jack-o'-lanterns she carves. They're amazing."

"The witch *made* you tell us that just to trick us," George insisted.

"Yeah," Benjamin agreed. "You're bewitched, Katie."

Katie shook her head. "No, I'm not. It's true. I saw the clocks and the pumpkins. And you can, too. Mrs. Hamilton wants us all to go to her house to trick-or-treat on Halloween."

"Are you nuts?" Kevin exclaimed. "I'm never going back there."

"Me either," George agreed.

Katie looked over at Emma W. "How about you?" she asked her. "We could go together."

Emma shook her head. "Sorry, Katie. I don't really like scary stuff like witches."

Katie shook her head sadly. Mrs. Hamilton was going to be so disappointed if no one came to her house the next day. And she was such a nice lady. The kids would really like her if they got to know her. If only Katie could find a way for them to meet her.

Out of the corner of her eye, Katie caught a glimpse of Mr. Guthrie walking into the school building. He was carrying some more

Halloween decorations to put up in class 4A, to get the room ready for tomorrow's Halloween celebration.

Just then, Katie got one of her great ideas. "Mr. Guthrie!" she shouted. "Wait up. I need to ask you something!"

Chapter 15

As Katie walked onto the playground the next morning, she could hear some of the kids talking about her. Well, not about her, actually. The person the kids were whispering about was Mrs. Hamilton. She'd met Katie on the playground. Now they were walking into the school building together.

"Isn't that the Witch of Elm Lane?" Katie heard Kevin whisper to George.

George nodded nervously as he stared at the tall woman in the long black coat. "She sure looks like her."

"Why is the witch going into our school?" Becky wondered.

"And why is Katie with her?" Jeremy asked. "I hope she's okay."

"I don't know. Katie looks kind of like a witch, too," Mandy pointed out. "I mean, she's dressed all in black, she's carrying a broom, and she's wearing that creepy cape."

"She's not supposed to wear that now! It's supposed to be for the parade!" Suzanne blurted out. She covered her mouth quickly. She'd just ruined her and Katie's Halloween surprise.

But the kids had bigger things to be concerned about than Suzanne's costume.

"Maybe the witch bit Katie on the neck and turned her into a witch, too," Benjamin suggested.

"That's vampires . . . again!" George reminded him. "Sheesh."

"Wow, Katie is really brave," Emma W. said. "She's the only person I know who would stand that close to a witch. I sure wouldn't. I'd be too scared."

Kadeem pointed to the huge object hidden inside a brown shopping bag. Mrs. Hamilton was holding the bag in her arms. "I think the Witch of Elm Lane is carrying a cauldron," he said.

"I wonder if she's going to boil up a witch's brew?" Isobel suggested.

"I'm *definitely* not eating anything they serve in the cafeteria today," Rachel said. "Who knows what will be in it?"

Katie tried hard not to laugh as she walked past the fourth- and fifth-graders. They were all acting like such scaredy-cats.

Still, the kids weren't all wrong. Mrs. Hamilton was about to do something almost magical inside the school.

And only Katie knew just what that was.

"Welcome, goblins," Mr. G. said as he greeted the kids in class 4A a few moments later. "Happy Halloween!"

Mr. G. was all dressed up for Halloween.

That didn't surprise his class, though. They'd seen their teacher in costumes before. He'd once come to school dressed as Abraham Lincoln to teach the kids about American history. And while they were studying ancient Egypt, he'd come dressed as King Tut. But this was the most amazing costume they'd ever seen him in.

Mr. G. was dressed as Frankenstein. He was wearing big black boots and a dark suit with big shoulders. He had on a black wig, and he'd painted big ugly scars on his face. He'd even attached two big rubber bolts to his neck.

But it wasn't Mr. G.'s costume that frightened the kids the most. They were all much more scared of Katie and Mrs. Hamilton. The two of them were standing in the far corner of the room in front of a table. There were knives of all sizes on the table. Beside the knives was a big black pot.

"She's going to cook us!" George shouted. He ran for the door.

Mr. G. stopped him. "George! That's not any way to treat a guest. Now sit back down and apologize," the teacher insisted.

George shook his head, hard. "I'm getting out of here," he insisted. "Now!"

"What's the matter, George?" Katie asked mysteriously. "Don't you want to see what we have in store for you?"

George gulped. "I . . . I . . . don't think so."

"Sure you do," Katie told him. "We're going to do something absolutely be*witch*ing."

"I want to get out of here," George insisted, shivering.

"George, sit down, now," Mr. G. told him strongly.

George bit his lower lip and did what he was told.

"Now, apologize to Katie and Mrs. Hamilton," Mr. G. continued.

"Sorry," George mumbled nervously under his breath.

Katie smiled strangely as she picked up a

small screwdriver-shaped knife and handed it to Mrs. Hamilton. "We're ready to begin."

Chapter 16

"Katie, will you please pull out the victim?" Mrs. Hamilton asked in a dark, mysterious, Halloween-like voice.

"Certainly," Katie replied with a grin. She reached down under the table.

"No, Katie, don't hurt anyone!" Kadeem cried out.

"Not me!" George said, burrowing himself down deep into his beanbag chair. "I don't want to be a victim!"

"Me neither!" Kevin shouted with a shudder.

"What's the matter with you guys?" Katie asked them. She pulled a big orange pumpkin out of the shopping bag beneath the table.

"Tha . . . that's your victim?" George asked. "A pumpkin?"

"Of course," Katie told him. "Mrs. Hamilton is going to show us how to carve fancy jack-o'-lanterns. What did you guys think we were doing?"

George blushed. "Nothing. I mean . . ."

"I told you Mrs. Hamilton carved amazing jack-o'-lanterns," Katie explained. "My mom and I went over to her house and watched her carve one last night. It was really cool."

Mr. G. smiled at his class. "Katie thought a pumpkin-carving demonstration would be a really special treat for Halloween. And speaking of treats . . ." The teacher walked over to the big black pot on the table. "When we're finished, we're going to toast the pumpkin seeds. You won't believe how delicious they're going to taste!"

"Oh, yum!" Emma W. said excitedly. "I love toasted pumpkin seeds. My mother makes them on Halloween, too. This was a great

idea, Katie."

"It sure was," George agreed. "Mrs. Hamilton, hurry up and show us how to carve a jack-o'-lantern, will you, please?"

"Why are you in such a hurry, George?" Katie asked him curiously.

"Because the sooner we carve, the sooner we get to snack on those seeds!"

Mrs. Hamilton cackled slightly. "George, you're absolutely right. Let's get started. First,

I'll take this paper pattern and pin it to the pumpkin."

The kids all watched as Mrs. Hamilton pinned a piece of paper onto the front of the pumpkin. Then she took a small knife and poked little holes along the lines she had drawn on the paper.

"It's very important to keep your pattern simple," Mrs. Hamilton told the kids. "That way you will make fewer mistakes."

"Where did you learn to do this?" Mandy asked her.

"My mother taught me when I was a little girl. She was an artist. A sculptor, actually. Usually she made statues from stone. But on Halloween she sculpted pumpkins, instead."

Katie smiled, remembering the beautiful sculpture of a mother and child inside Mrs. Hamilton's house. Her mother must have made it.

"What kind of jack-o'-lanterns do you have at your house?" Emma S. asked Mrs.

Hamilton.

"This year I've made a cat, a skeleton, a bat, and a ghost," Mrs. Hamilton told them.

"I'd sure like to see those," Emma W. said.

"Me too," Kadeem agreed.

"Well, they'll be out on my front porch tonight," Mrs. Hamilton told the kids. "I hope you'll all come by and see them while you're trick-or-treating."

"We sure will," George said excitedly. He was obviously not afraid of Mrs. Hamilton anymore.

"We should tell the kids in 4B about the jack-o'-lanterns," Emma S. suggested. "Maybe they'll come see them, too."

Katie smiled. Her friends weren't afraid of Mrs. Hamilton anymore. Her plan had worked!

Mrs. Hamilton carved really quickly. She'd obviously had a lot of practice at making jack-o'-lanterns. In about half an hour, she was finished.

"Okay, that should just about do it," she told the kids. She reached into her bag and pulled out a long white candle. She placed it inside the center of the jack-o'-lantern. "Okay, Mr. Guthrie," she said. "You can turn out the lights."

Mr. Guthrie flicked the switch. The room went dark.

"Ta-da!" Mrs. Hamilton announced as she turned the pumpkin around.

The pumpkin had a girl's face carved into it. The girl had big round eyes, a bright smile, and pigtails.

"It's me!" Katie told the class proudly.

"It sure is," Mrs. Hamilton agreed. "I hope you like it."

"I love it!" Katie exclaimed. "In fact, this is the best Halloween treat I've ever gotten!"

Chapter 17

"Katie, there you are," Suzanne shouted as Katie made her way over to where the fourth-graders were lining up in the school yard for the Halloween parade later that day. "I didn't think you were going to make it."

"Sorry I'm late," Katie said, apologizing. "This green makeup was harder to put on than I thought it would be."

"It looks great, though," Suzanne complimented her. "Really scary." She twirled around so her lacy skirt blew all around her. "How do you like *my* costume?"

"It's beautiful," Katie told her. "You look a lot like the Glinda in the movie. I really love that crown."

"Me too," Suzanne agreed. "It's so glittery. And it matches my wand." She studied Katie's costume. "Hey, where's your broom?"

"Oh, no!" Katie moaned. "I must have left it in the classroom."

"Well, you'd better run back and get it," Suzanne insisted. "You can't be the Wicked Witch of the West without your broom. That's the most important prop in the whole movie! Except for the ruby slippers that *I* give Dorothy, of course." Suzanne smiled proudly.

"You're not really Glinda," Katie teased Suzanne.

Suzanne rolled her eyes. "I know. Now go get your broom. We only have a few minutes."

"Okay," Katie agreed. She turned and headed back toward the building.

As Katie neared the school, she heard a familiar sound. *"Mew. Mew."* Quickly, she turned around. There was the black kitten she'd been seeing all around town.

"Are you following me?" Katie whispered.

The cat looked back at her with its big green eyes.

"Well, don't worry. As soon as this contest is over, I'll get you a big saucer of milk," Katie promised the cat. "But right now, I've got to get going."

The school building was completely silent as Katie went inside. Everybody was already outside waiting for the parade to begin.

Katie hurried toward class 4A so she could get her broom. But before she could reach her classroom, she felt a cool breeze blowing on the back of her neck. She raised the collar on her cape, trying to block the draft.

But a cloth cape was no match for this wind. After all, it was no ordinary wind. It was the *magic* wind.

Within seconds the magic wind picked up speed, blowing harder and harder until it was a wild tornado blowing only around Katie. *Whoosh!* The magic wind was so powerful that

Katie was sure it would blow her away. She shut her eyes tight and tried not to cry.

And then it stopped. Just like that. The magic wind was gone.

Katie sighed. She knew what that meant. Katie had been switcherooed. Now she was somebody else.

The question was . . . who?

Chapter 18

Katie opened her big green eyes slowly and looked around. She blinked slightly with surprise as the images around her came into focus.

Boy, that's weird, she thought to herself. *The grass looks green and the sky looks blue, but everything else looks kind of gray.*

Katie rubbed her eyes with her front paws and looked around again.

Wait a minute, she thought. *Paws? I don't have paws!*

She looked down at where her hands were supposed to be. All she saw were two tiny black paws.

Cat paws!

"Oh, no!" Katie shouted. "I don't want to be a cat! Not now. Not before the parade!"

But all that came out of her mouth was *"Meow! Meow! Meow!"*

Just then, Katie spotted a little sparrow flying out of a nearby tree. It landed on the playground and began nibbling on a piece of a cookie someone had dropped there.

Katie didn't want to chase the bird. She really didn't. But she was *so* hungry. She couldn't help herself.

Katie ran over to the bird. She was amazed at just how quietly and gracefully she could move. The bird didn't even seem to know she was there. Katie moved closer and closer. She spread her claws and got ready to . . .

"AAAAH! It's a black cat!" Suzanne screamed. She ran as far from Katie as she could.

"Don't let it cross your path!" Jessica Haynes added, following after Suzanne. She had a hard time running in her big rubber clown shoes.

"Achoo!" Sam McDonough sneezed from behind his monster mask. "I'm allergic to cats!"

"Keep that black cat away from me!" Emma S. said, dashing across the playground in her red, white, and blue American flag outfit. "I worked too hard on this costume to get bad luck now."

"I didn't work on my costume at all," Kadeem told her, pointing to his own store-bought Joker costume. "But I don't want any bad luck, either."

It seemed to Katie that everyone was screaming very, very loudly! Her little kitten ears were ringing with noise. She had to get out of there.

"*Meowwwww!*" she howled as she raced away from the school yard. She just had to find some peace and quiet.

114

The quietest place Katie could think of was her own backyard. She knew nobody would be home. Both of her parents were at work. So were her neighbors, Mr. and Mrs. Derkman. Mr. Derkman was at the office, and Mrs. Derkman was at school watching the parade with all the other Cherrydale Elementary School teachers.

Katie wished she could be back at school, too. She had really wanted to be part of that Halloween parade. But she knew she couldn't be there now. All the kids were afraid of her. And besides, this black kitten suit was a lot more than just a costume. Katie really was a kitten. At least until the magic wind came back, anyway.

Katie walked quickly through the tall grass. Her stomach grumbled as she walked along. She was so hungry that even the thought of eating a mouse sounded good to her.

How disgusting was that?!

Katie purred sadly.

I'm never, ever going to listen to Suzanne again, she vowed to herself. *I should have fed the kitten when I had the chance.*

A few minutes later, some familiar houses came into view. Katie had found her way back to her own block. She was almost home.

Katie moved her four little feet as fast as she could. Finally, she reached her front yard.

Katie could feel herself getting excited as she spotted the big tree in front of her house. Suddenly, she had an overwhelming need to scratch at the tree. She didn't know why. She just knew that there was nothing else she would rather do at that moment than scratch and scratch and scratch at the wood.

As soon as Katie reached the tree, her claws popped out from her front paws. She stood up on her hind legs and began to scratch at the bark.

"Aaaahh," Katie purred contentedly as she felt the soft wood of the tree under her claws.

Scratch, scratch, scratch. She couldn't believe how much fun this was. Katie scratched harder and harder. She purred and purred.

Honk! Honk!

A car horn beeped in the distance. Ordinarily, Katie wouldn't have even noticed it. But to Katie's sensitive cat ears, the horn sounded very, very loud.

How weird, Katie thought. Suddenly, it was kind of scary just to be outside—even in her own yard. Katie felt so small. And everything else seemed so loud and large.

Maybe it was best to go inside her house. At least she knew she would be safe there.

Katie raced onto the porch and squeezed herself through the open downstairs window. She landed in her living room. Quickly, she scampered over to the couch and curled up on a soft pillow.

Mmm . . . it felt so warm and cozy . . .

"Ruff! Ruff! AROOOOOOO!"

Katie's ears perked up, and her whiskers

suddenly twitched. There was danger coming. She could sense it.

"RRRRRUFFFFFFFFF!"

Oh, no! Katie had forgotten all about Pepper. How could she have not remembered her own dog? What a strange day this had become.

"Grrrrrr!" Pepper growled angrily in Katie's direction.

Katie gulped.

This was *so* not good!

Chapter 19

"Pepper, get away from me!" Katie shouted at her dog.

Pepper stopped for a moment and cocked his brown and white head, listening. Katie could tell he sensed something was different about this cat.

"That's it, Pepper. You know it's me, don't you, boy?" Katie said quietly.

Pepper looked at the kitten curiously. He was obviously trying to figure out what was going on.

"That's right, it's me," Katie purred to him. "You're the only one who can recognize me when the magic wind does its switcheroos."

Pepper may have suspected that the kitten was really Katie, but that didn't change the fact that he was still a dog and she was still a cat.

"Grrrrrr," Pepper growled again as he raced in her direction.

"Oh, no!" Katie meowed. She quickly leaped up onto the windowsill. Then she squeezed her way out of the house and back into the yard.

The window was only open by a small crack. A tiny kitten could fit through it, but a big cocker spaniel couldn't.

Still, just to be sure Pepper didn't find some other way to get out of the house and come after her, Katie climbed up the tree and balanced herself on a branch. No dog could get her up there.

Pepper leaped up onto the couch and scratched at the window.

"Aroo! Aroo!" Pepper howled.

"Pepper, stop it!" Katie hissed down to

him. "Mom's going to be mad if you leave marks on the window!"

But Pepper wouldn't listen. He just stood there barking and barking at the Katie-cat in the tree.

Katie couldn't believe it. She was being barked at by her own dog. The magic wind sure had made a mess of things this time!

Still, she felt pretty safe up in the tree. And it was kind of comfortable up there. "This sun feels really good right now," she purred.

She stretched out her long black body and let the sunlight warm her tired back and legs. Then she reached down with her rough pink tongue and began licking her paws.

Blech. Small pieces of black hair got caught on the rough parts of her tongue. They tickled and itched as they slid down her throat.

This is disgusting, Katie thought. *I can't believe I'm licking my own feet! And I'm going to get a fur ball stuck in my throat if I don't stop swallowing all this hair.*

But she kept on licking. After all, she was a cat now. And that's what cats did. They licked themselves clean.

Finally, Pepper grew tired of barking at the kitten in the tree. Katie figured he was hot and thirsty from all the barking.

Now that Pepper was quiet, Katie decided to leave. She stood up on all fours and gave a little push on her back paws. In a moment, she was in the air, leaping from the tree branch to the grass below.

As she moved through the air she straightened her body, positioning her legs so that they would be the first things to hit the ground when she landed. A moment later, she was standing on the ground, her body ready to run.

As she raced through Cherrydale, Katie leaped up on fences, then pounced down to the ground. She pushed herself to jump farther and farther.

Wow, it would be nice to be able to jump this

far when I'm human, she thought. *I could be the star long jumper on the school track team!*

A few minutes later, Katie stopped her running and jumping and stood still. She opened her mouth slightly and smelled the air.

"How weird is this?" Katie meowed softly. "I'm smelling with the roof of my mouth!"

No matter how she might be doing it, Katie knew exactly what she was smelling. Meat! Delicious meat! And it was coming from that trash can over there.

If she had been a fourth-grade girl again, Katie would have been totally grossed out at the idea of eating from a trash can. And she certainly wouldn't be eating meat! But Katie wasn't a fourth-grade girl. She was a kitten. A very hungry kitten.

"Meow!" Katie shouted excitedly as she dashed over to the trash can.

But before she could reach the meat, Katie was stopped by a tall woman in a black coat. The woman scooped her up in her arms.

"It's you again," the woman said in a crackly voice.

Katie looked up at her. It was Mrs. Hamilton!

"You can't make a meal out of my garbage," the old woman said as she gently stroked Katie's fur. "Come. I'll take you someplace where you can get a proper meal."

Chapter 20

"Okay, little one," a man with a gentle voice said as he placed Katie down on a soft table covered with white paper. "You stay here, and I'll be right back."

"*Meow,*" Katie replied nervously as the man walked out of the room and shut the door behind him.

Katie was scared. Mrs. Hamilton had put her in her car and driven her to this place. After they'd gone inside, she'd handed her over to the man.

And then he'd left her all alone in this cold little room with no windows and only one door. Katie felt scared and trapped.

"Meow!" she shouted out nervously as she leaped from the table to the floor, searching for a way out.

But there was nowhere to go. There was just the one door. And that was closed.

Katie began to paw nervously at a wooden cat tree in the corner of the room. She scratched and scratched, going around and around the wooden post until she spotted a small metal bowl of water in another corner of the room.

Katie was one very thirsty kitten. She stopped scratching the post, padded over to the water, and began lapping it up.

As she was drinking, Katie's whiskers began to move slightly. They could sense that something was changing in the air. A slight breeze had begun to blow.

Within seconds the breeze turned into a strong wind. Before long it was a tornado, spinning and spinning right around Katie.

"MEOW!" Katie shouted out nervously.

The tornado whirled around and around.

And then it stopped. Just like that.

The magic wind was gone.

Katie opened her eyes. Her face was stuck in a bowl of water, and she was lapping the water up with her tongue! She could see the floor between her four paws.

Oh, no. Had the magic wind forgotten to change her back into herself?

Then Katie looked again. Wait a minute. Those weren't her paws. They were her hands. She could tell, because her nails were painted black for the Halloween parade.

"Mew. Mew."

Suddenly, Katie noticed the frightened little black kitten hiding behind the table. Not only was Katie back to her old self, the kitten was, too. And she seemed very, very scared.

Katie spotted a pad of paper on the table next to where the cat was standing. The address on top of the pad read: Cherrydale Animal Shelter. Now Katie knew where she was.

"Don't worry, little kitten," Katie told the small black cat. "They will take good care of you here."

The shelter was a good place for animals to stay, but a kid belonged in school. Katie had to get back there—and fast—before anyone noticed she was missing.

But that meant she also had to sneak out of the shelter without anyone seeing her. There was no way she'd be able to explain how she got in here. No one would believe her, even if she told them.

Katie opened the door of the room very slightly—just enough so she could see out into the lobby. She peeked out and checked to see if anybody was out there.

The coast was clear. It seemed all the veterinarians and helpers at the shelter were working with the animals. This was the perfect time for Katie to sneak away without anyone seeing her.

"I've got to go," Katie told the kitten. "But don't you worry. I'll be back."

Chapter 21

"There you are, Katie!" Suzanne shouted as Katie raced back onto the playground. "Where have you been? You missed the whole parade."

"Well, I . . . um . . ." Katie stammered. She didn't know what to say.

"It sure took you a long time to find that broom," Suzanne noted.

Katie shrugged. "I know. I went into the classroom to look for it and I . . . well . . . I sort of got stuck for a while."

"You mean the door locked all by itself?" Suzanne asked.

Katie sighed. That was as good of an

explanation as any. "Must have been the wind," she murmured.

That wasn't a lie. A wind did keep her away from the parade. A really big wind . . . the magic wind!

"It doesn't matter, anyway," Suzanne assured her. She held up a little silver plastic trophy. "They gave out all different sorts of prizes this year, instead of just one. I won the prize for prettiest costume."

"That is a really amazing fairy princess costume," Jessica said, coming over to compliment Suzanne.

"No, she's supposed to be Gli—" Katie began.

"I'm a *fairy princess*," Suzanne insisted, shooting Katie a look. "That's what the judges said."

"Oh," Katie said, nodding with understanding. She wouldn't tell anyone who Suzanne was really supposed to be.

"What happened to your witch makeup?"

Suzanne asked Katie. "It's all smeared. It looks like you stuck your head in a big bucket of water."

"It was a bowl of water, actually," Katie said without thinking. Then she stopped herself. "Just kidding. Actually, I think the makeup's sweating off."

"Oh, well, you can put more on before we go trick-or-treating tonight," Suzanne told her. "Too bad we couldn't win an award together. But you can come over and look at *my* trophy anytime you want."

"Gee, thanks," Katie said sarcastically.

"Oh, here comes Jeremy," Suzanne sighed. "He's probably going to start bragging all about his trophy. I can't stand it when people do that. I'll see you later."

As Suzanne walked off, Katie laughed. Suzanne bragged more than anyone else in the fourth grade.

"Hi, Katie," Jeremy said, walking over to her. "Where were you? I didn't see you in the parade."

"Oh, I've been around," Katie told him. She looked at the gold trophy in his hand. "What did you win for?"

"Most original costume," Jeremy told her proudly.

"Congratulations," Katie said. "That's awesome!"

Just then, Jeremy's Aunt Sheila came walking over toward them with her car keys in her hand. At least, Katie thought it was his Aunt Sheila. It was hard to tell underneath the beautiful bird mask she was wearing.

"Hi there, Jeremy!" the woman in the bird mask called out.

Katie smiled. It was definitely Jeremy's Aunt Sheila.

"Hi, Aunt Sheila!" Jeremy greeted her. "What are you doing here?"

"I came to pick you up after the parade. I was dying to see if you won."

Jeremy proudly held up his trophy. "I sure

did!" he exclaimed. "I was afraid I wasn't going to, though. Especially after this black cat ran across the playground."

"Oh, Jeremy, you know black cats don't cause bad luck," his Aunt Sheila insisted. "I love them. There was a tiny stray black cat in the neighborhood that I used to feed when I was a little girl. She was just the cutest thing."

"Did Jeremy's mom like the black cat, too?" Katie asked curiously.

"Oh, yes," Jeremy's aunt recalled with a smile. "We both adored her."

"What happened to her?" Jeremy asked.

His Aunt Sheila shrugged. "I guess she got adopted or something, because after a while, she stopped coming around for food. We really missed her."

Katie began to smile. She was getting another one of her great ideas.

"You know, there's a really cute black kitten at the Cherrydale Animal Shelter

137

that would just *love* to be adopted," she told Jeremy and his aunt.

Jeremy shook his head. "My mom would never go for it."

"But maybe if she went down to the shelter and saw the kitten, it would remind her of the cat she and your Aunt Sheila used to feed," Katie suggested. "Then she might feel differently."

"I'll bet she would," Jeremy's aunt agreed. "She was really crazy about that black stray in our old neighborhood."

"It's worth a try," Jeremy said.

"I'll call your mom and tell her to meet us over at the animal shelter," Aunt Sheila said. She turned to Katie. "Would you like to come with us?"

"Would I ever!" Katie exclaimed.

"Great," Aunt Sheila said. "You can call your mom from the car and let her know where you'll be."

"I'm so glad you're coming," Jeremy told

Katie. "It's going to take all three of us to convince my mom to let me get that kitten."

Chapter 22

"I'm not sure how you kids found out about the black kitten being here," Dr. Bader, the veterinarian at the Cherrydale Animal Shelter, told Katie and Jeremy. "She was just brought in this afternoon."

"Yeah, how did you know about the kitten?" Jeremy asked Katie curiously.

"I . . . um . . ." Katie stammered, not sure what to say. "Well, you see, I've sort of been seeing her around the neighborhood for a couple of days, and I was pretty sure someone would have brought her here by now."

"Oh," Jeremy said. "That makes sense."

Phew, Katie sighed. That was a close one.

"Well, you were right," Dr. Bader told Katie. "A nice woman brought her here earlier. And it was a good thing, too. This little kitty has been out on the streets for a while now, I think. She was very hungry."

"And thirsty, too," Katie added.

Everyone stared at her.

"I mean, I would guess that she was thirsty," she said, blushing.

"Did you give her a saucer of milk?" Jeremy asked Dr. Bader.

"Oh, no," the veterinarian told him. "Milk can actually give a cat an upset stomach. We gave her water and some cat food, though. Now all she needs is a good home where she can get a lot of love."

"Oh, our home is a very good home," Jeremy assured Dr. Bader as he followed her into the special room where the kittens that were waiting to be adopted lived. "And we all love one another. Don't we, Mom?"

"Now, Jeremy," his mother reminded him,

"I said I'd look at the kitten. I didn't say we'd be bringing her home."

"Oh, you're going to love her, Mrs. Fox," Katie told Jeremy's mother. "She's the sweetest kitten."

"We'll see," Mrs. Fox said. But she didn't sound very convinced.

"Ah, here she is," Dr. Bader said. She stopped at a small cage in the back of the room. The little black kitten was huddled in the back of the cage.

"Oh, my, she looks just like the kitten we used to feed behind our house," Jeremy's aunt said.

"She really does," Mrs. Fox agreed. "She even has the same big green eyes. And look at her tiny pink nose."

Katie smiled. Those did not sound like the words of someone who didn't want a pet.

Dr. Bader opened up the cage and gently reached inside. Slowly, she took the kitten out and held her up to Jeremy.

"Would you like to hold her?" she asked him.

"Oh! Can I?" Jeremy asked.

"Sure," Dr. Bader said. She placed the kitten gently into Jeremy's arms.

Jeremy began petting the cat's fur. "She's so soft," he said quietly. The kitten purred contentedly as Jeremy petted her.

"I think she likes you," Katie said excitedly.

"I think so, too," Jeremy agreed.

"Is this kitten healthy?" Jeremy's mother asked.

Dr. Bader nodded. "We've run some tests, and everything seems fine."

"Do you want to hold her, Mom?" Jeremy asked, holding the kitten out to his mother.

"Well, I don't know . . ." Mrs. Fox began.

"Oh, go ahead, Emily," Jeremy's Aunt Sheila suggested. "We were never allowed to hold the stray cats around our house." She looked at Katie and Jeremy. "Our mother wouldn't let us," she explained.

"Well, all right," Mrs. Fox said, taking the kitten from Jeremy's arms. She held her just like a baby. "My, she is soft."

"Your mother was right not to let you touch stray cats," Dr. Bader told Jeremy's aunt. "Some stray cats can have diseases. And others can be pretty mean—especially if they're afraid. This happens to be a very gentle kitten."

"That's a good kind of kitten for a kid to adopt, isn't it?" Katie asked Dr. Bader hopefully.

"The best kind," the veterinarian agreed.

"Look how sweet she is, Mom," Jeremy said.

"Oh, she's cuddling up to your neck," his aunt added. "You have to admit you like that."

"I can help Jeremy take care of her," Katie told Mrs. Fox. "I have lots of experience with animals."

Mrs. Fox sighed. "Well, I can't fight all three of you," she said slowly.

The kitten purred.

"Make that all *four* of you," Mrs. Fox corrected herself with a laugh. She turned to Jeremy. "And you'll be sure to feed her and give her water?"

Jeremy nodded. "I'll even clean her litter box."

"Wow," Aunt Sheila said. "That's pretty impressive."

Mrs. Fox sighed heavily and handed the kitten back to Jeremy. "Well then, I guess we have a new member of the family," she said. She reached into her bag and pulled out her cell phone. "I'd better call and warn your dad. I don't want him to be surprised when he walks into the house and finds cat toys in the living room."

"Make sure you get a scratching post," Katie suggested, remembering how good it had felt to scratch at the tree in her front yard. "I know the kitten will love that."

"So, what are you going to name your new

friend?" Dr. Bader asked Jeremy.

Jeremy stared at his kitten for a while. "I think I'll call her Lucky," he said finally. He smiled at Katie. "Because she and I are so lucky to have each other."

Katie smiled broadly. "That's perfect!" she exclaimed.

Chapter 23

"Lucky has got the softest fur," Jeremy told the other kids that evening as they walked around Cherrydale trick-or-treating. "I didn't want to put her down to eat dinner. But my mom made me."

Katie smiled as she listened to Jeremy telling everyone about his new kitten. He had wanted a pet for so long. And now he had one. Katie knew how wonderful that could be.

"I can't wait to introduce Lucky to Pepper," Jeremy said to Katie. "I'll bet they'll be best friends, just like we are."

Katie tried not to laugh. She knew that wasn't going to happen. At least not right away.

"I don't know," she told him. "A dog and a cat can be trouble together. Pepper will probably start barking. And Lucky will get upset and climb up a tree or something."

"Oh, I don't think so," Jeremy insisted. "Sure, some cats and dogs fight. But not Pepper and Lucky. They're different."

Wanna bet? Katie thought. But she didn't say anything.

"Well, I can't believe you adopted a black cat," Suzanne said as she lugged her bag of candy down the block.

"And I can't believe you took seven pieces of candy from Mr. Brigandi's candy bowl," George told her.

Suzanne shrugged. "He said 'Take whatever you want,'" she explained. "So I did."

"I think it was very brave of Jeremy to adopt a black cat," Becky told Suzanne. "Even unlucky animals need homes."

"Lucky is not unlucky," Jeremy told her angrily.

"Oh, you know what I mean," Becky said. "I'm not afraid of Lucky. I can't wait to meet her!" She smiled at him as she fixed her football helmet and pads. Becky had dressed as a football player for Halloween. "Come on, let's go to the next house." She ran up the steps and rang the doorbell.

"I'll bet Lucky won't like *her*," Jeremy groaned. "Why can't Becky just leave me alone?"

George laughed and lifted up his one-eyed monster mask. "We sure collected a lot of candy tonight," he told the others. "Much more than I ever would have gotten back in my old neighborhood."

"I'm never going to be able to eat all this candy," Emma W. admitted. She smiled through her white bridal veil. "Good thing I have so many people in my house to share it with."

"I guess a big family can come in handy sometimes," Katie said. "I can't share my candy with Pepper. Candy is terrible for dogs.

Especially chocolate."

"Cats too," Jeremy said. He smiled at Katie. "That's something else Lucky and Pepper have in common!"

Katie nodded. Jeremy really wanted their pets to be friends. Well, maybe they could. Pepper could change his mind about Lucky. After all, stranger things had happened . . . lots of times!

"Okay, let's fly over to Mrs. Hamilton's house," Mrs. Carew suggested. Katie's mom had used the extra black material from Katie's dress and cape to make herself a bat costume. She waved her arms up and down so her bat wings looked like they were flying.

"Yeah!" Kevin cheered from underneath the white sheet that was his ghost costume. "I can't wait to see those jack-o'-lanterns!"

"Especially the one of the cat," Jeremy added.

Suzanne groaned. "Are you going to talk about that kitten the whole time we're trick-

or-treating?"

Jeremy smiled at her. "Yep!"

Suzanne sighed. "It's going to be a long night."

"There's Mrs. Hamilton's house," George shouted, running up to the door. "Wow! Those pumpkins are so cool!"

"I'm glad you like them, George," Mrs. Hamilton said as she walked out onto her porch.

Katie stared at her in amazement. Mrs. Hamilton was dressed in a long, flowing dress. She was wearing a blond wig and lots of makeup. "Wow," Katie told her. "You look like a movie star."

"Yeah," George agreed. "You don't look like a witch at all!"

"George!" Katie exclaimed. "That's not nice!"

But Mrs. Hamilton laughed. "I hope not," she told George with a grin. "Now, I'll bet you kids want something, don't you?"

"Oh, yeah," Kevin said. "I almost forgot." He held out his bag. "Trick or treat!"

As Mrs. Hamilton placed a chocolate bar in Kevin's bag, Katie began to feel a cool breeze blowing on her neck.

Oh, no! she thought nervously. *Not now. Not tonight when I'm having so much fun. I don't want to be switcherooed tonight. I just want to be Katie. Well, Katie dressed as a witch. But Katie just the same.*

"Oh, my, it's getting a little windy," Mrs. Hamilton remarked. "I think I'm going to have to get my shawl."

Katie breathed a sigh of relief. If Mrs. Hamilton felt the wind, then it couldn't be the magic wind. It was just a regular old, every-day, run-of-the-mill kind of wind.

Katie had nothing to worry about. She could concentrate on what was most important on Halloween night.

She held out her bag and smiled at Mrs. Hamilton. "Trick or treat!" she said happily.

DISCARD
NORMAL PUBLIC LIBRARY
NORMAL, ILLINOIS

About the Author

NANCY KRULIK is the author of more than 150 books for children and young adults, including three *New York Times* bestsellers. She lives in New York City with her husband, composer Daniel Burwasser, their children, Amanda and Ian, and Pepper, a chocolate and white spaniel mix. When she's not busy writing the *Katie Kazoo, Switcheroo* series, Nancy loves swimming, reading, and going to the movies. Halloween is Nancy's favorite holiday—she just loves filling her apartment with skeletons, ghosts, goblins, and sticky spiderwebs. But Nancy's apartment isn't really haunted . . . or at least she doesn't think so!

✕ ✕ ✕

About the Illustrators

JOHN & WENDY'S art has been featured in other books for children, in magazines, on stationery, and on toys. When they are not drawing Katie and her friends, they like to paint, take photographs, travel, and play music in their rock-n-roll band. They live and work in Brooklyn, NY.